Princess Ponies

Best Friends Forever!

The Princess Ponies series

Princess Ponies ♘

Best Friends Forever!

CHLOE RYDER

BLOOMSBURY

NEW YORK LONDON OXFORD NEW DELHI SYDNEY

First published in Great Britain in January 2014 by Bloomsbury Publishing Plc
Published in the United States of America in January 2015
by Bloomsbury Children's Books
www.bloomsbury.com

Bloomsbury is a registered trademark of Bloomsbury Publishing Plc

For information about permission to reproduce selections from this book, write to
Permissions, Bloomsbury Children's Books, 1385 Broadway, New York, New York 10018
Bloomsbury books may be purchased for business or promotional use. For information on
bulk purchases please contact Macmillan Corporate and Premium Sales Department at
specialmarkets@macmillan.com

Library of Congress Cataloging-in-Publication Data
Ryder, Chloe.
Best friends forever! / by Chloe Ryder.
pages   cm.   — (Princess ponies ; 6)
Summary: The Royal Ponies join Pippa and her best friend, princess pony Stardust, in their
search to find the final golden horseshoe needed to save the enchanted island of Chevalia.
ISBN 978-1-61963-405-3 (paperback) • ISBN 978-1-61963-406-0 (e-book)
[1. Ponies—Fiction. 2. Magic—Fiction. 3. Princesses—Fiction. 4. Best friends—Fiction.
5. Friendship—Fiction.] I. Title. II. Title: Best friends forever!
PZ7.R95898Be 2014   [Fic]—dc23   2014006140

Typeset by Hewer Text UK Ltd, Edinburgh
Printed in China by Leo Paper Products, Heshan, Guangdong
6 8 10 9 7 5

For Lucy, Jessica, Andrew, and Harry

With special thanks to Julie Sykes

The Pony

Queen
Moonshine

Princess
Crystal

Princess
Cloud

Princess
Stardust

Princess
Honey

Royal Family

King Firestar

Prince Jet

Prince Comet

Prince Storm

Cloud
Forest

Volcano

Wild Forest

Stableside
Castle

Early one morning, just before dawn, two ponies stood in an ancient court-yard, looking sadly at a stone wall.

"In all my life this wall has never been empty. I can't believe that the horse-shoes have been taken—and just before Midsummer Day too," said the stallion.

He was a handsome animal—a copper-colored pony, with strong legs and bright eyes, dressed in a royal red sash.

The mare was a dainty yet majestic palomino with a golden coat and a pure white tail that fell to the ground like a waterfall.

She whinnied softly. "We don't have much time to find them all."

With growing sadness the two ponies watched the night fade away and the sun rise. When the first ray of sunlight spread into the courtyard it lit up the wall, showing the imprints where the golden horseshoes should have been hanging.

"Midsummer Day is the longest day of the year," said the stallion quietly. "It's the time when our ancient horseshoes must renew their magical energy. If the horseshoes are still missing in eight days, then by nightfall on the eighth day, their magic will fade and our beautiful island will be no more."

Sighing heavily, he touched his nose to his queen's.

"Only a miracle can save us now," he said.

The queen dipped her head, the diamonds on her crown sparkling in the early morning light.

"Have faith," she said gently. "I sense that a miracle is coming."

Chapter 1

A high-pitched cry woke Pippa. Throwing the covers back, she was out of bed even before she'd properly opened her eyes. In the enormous bed opposite hers, Princess Stardust was tossing about, thrashing her hooves and sobbing like a little foal.

Pippa went to comfort her best friend.

"Stardust, what's wrong?"

"No," Stardust cried, her breath coming in noisy snorts.

Gently, Pippa shook her friend awake.

"It's all right," she soothed. "You're safe now. It was just a bad dream."

Stardust struggled up, sleepily squinting at Pippa through the darkness as if she couldn't quite remember who she was. Pippa smoothed a tangle of white hair away from the princess pony's eyes.

"Better now?" she asked.

Stardust nuzzled at Pippa's hand.

"I was dreaming," she said flatly. "It was awful. It was Midsummer Day and we hadn't found all the missing horseshoes. The moment the sun set everything went completely black and there was a terrible roaring sound. Stableside Castle collapsed and the island shriveled up, leaving nothing but a lump of volcanic rock. All the ponies were huddled together on a tiny piece of land surrounded by the sea. The tide was coming in, swirling around our hooves and rising quickly up our legs. There was nowhere to go to escape the water. Baroness Divine had wings and she flew over us, shrieking with laughter and telling us that from now on we must wear hoods and not tiaras."

Stardust stumbled out of bed, picked up a comb, and halfheartedly tugged it through her mane.

"We're not going to let that happen!" Pippa said, taking the comb

7

and brushing Stardust's mane with long, calming strokes.

"You're such a good friend," Stardust neighed. "And perhaps we *can* find the last horseshoe."

Pippa hugged Stardust and walked over to the tower window.

"It's dawn," she said, pointing at the streaks of pink that stained the dark sky.

Stardust picked up her pink jeweled tiara from the dresser and hurriedly placed it on her head between her ears. Grabbing a towel, she gave her hooves a quick polish. Usually Stardust spent ages getting ready, so Pippa could tell that the nightmare had really frightened her.

Pippa reached for the clothes that

had magically appeared overnight and were laid out in a neat pile on the dresser—her new outfit was a pretty striped top and leggings.

"I'm ready," Pippa said, shoving her feet into sandals.

Stardust hesitated at the bedroom door.

"Pippa," she whispered, her brown eyes suddenly looking too large for her face. "What if we don't find it in time?"

"We will," Pippa said, her confident tone masking her own fear, "if we work together!"

Six days ago Pippa had just arrived at the seaside for a vacation with her family when two giant seahorses magically whisked her away to Chevalia, an island inhabited by talking ponies. There she had learned that the enchanted island was in grave danger. Eight golden horseshoes were supposed to hang on an ancient wall in the castle's courtyard. Every Midsummer Day the horseshoes' magical energy was renewed by the sun, ensuring that the island continued

to thrive. But the horseshoes had been
stolen and Pippa learned that it was her
quest to find them and bring them
home in time for Midsummer Day. If
she failed, Chevalia would fade away.

With Stardust's help she had managed
to find seven of the missing horseshoes,
but now Midsummer Day was here and
if Pippa didn't find the last one before
sunset then it would all have been for
nothing. Fear gripped her stomach like
an icy hand. Leading the way out of
the bedroom, she started to run down
the tower's spiral ramp.

"Breakfast first," Stardust said, nosing
open the dining room door.

Pippa was desperate to get going,
but Stardust was right—they needed a

good breakfast before beginning their final search.

Pippa was surprised to find that they weren't the only early birds—Stardust's brothers and sisters were already at their feeding troughs. No one seemed to be eating much, though. Princess Crystal rolled an apple around three times without even taking a bite, and Prince Comet's hot oatmeal grew cold while he listlessly flicked through a book.

"It's the last day today," Princess Honey said bravely, as Pippa and Stardust squeezed in beside her.

"Please don't start to worry yet," Pippa said.

She was shocked by Honey's untidy

appearance. Pretty Honey usually took such care of herself and was a regular customer at the Mane Street Salon, but this morning her mane was tangled and she wasn't wearing any hoof polish.

Pippa ate a dish of fresh fruit salad without tasting any of it.

"We should go up the Volcano today," she declared. "I bet that's where Divine has hidden the last horseshoe."

Yesterday Stardust and Pippa discovered that it was Baroness Divine, one of the queen's advisers, who had stolen the horseshoes. She foolishly believed that she could make a better life for herself without the Royal Ponies.

"That's if she hasn't already destroyed the horseshoe," Stardust said sadly.

Comet snapped his book shut. "I don't understand it. I thought every adult pony had read the ancient scrolls, but clearly Divine hasn't," he said. "If she had read them then she'd know how, a long time ago, Chevalia was little more than a volcano surrounded by the sea. It's the eight golden horseshoes that allowed it to grow into the wonderful island it is today, and they must have their magical energy renewed for all our sakes."

"Peggy told me that story yesterday," said Pippa. "She also mentioned her friend Nightingale, the scientist-magician."

Comet nodded. "Yes, it was Nightingale who discovered the magical gold buried in the volcanic rock. She used it to fashion the horseshoes."

"Mom used to tell me that story at bedtime, but I thought it was just a story for little foals." Stardust stared around the dining room. "Where is Mom? Is she still in bed?"

"Mom and Dad were up long before us," Crystal answered. "I think they went to the courtyard."

"Let's go and find them," Stardust said, leaving most of her breakfast untouched.

Queen Moonshine and King Firestar were indeed in the courtyard, standing close together and staring sadly at the ancient Whispering Wall. Seven horse-shoes sparkled in the early morning sun, but in spite of their brightness, Pippa's eyes were drawn to the gap where the eighth horseshoe should have been hanging. The bare space made her feel like a failure.

A shadow fell over the courtyard. Glancing up, Pippa saw Princess Cloud hovering above her in the air.

Queen Moonshine called out a greeting to her daughter, and Cloud swooped lower, making sure she kept her hooves away from the stone floor,

because touching down would mean losing her wings.

"I've got a plan," the queen said urgently. "Cloud, if you rub noses with every pony on the island then, come sunset, when the island begins to fade, everyone could fly away to safety."

"But that would take Cloud ages," squeaked Stardust.

"And where would the ponies go?" asked Pippa.

"They could find homes in the human world," the queen said.

Pippa shook her head. "Many of the ponies came here from the human world because they were neglected or treated badly there. We can't send them back again. And it isn't over yet—there's still time to find the last missing horseshoe."

"Pippa MacDonald, you've already faced so many dangers in your quest, and Chevalia is already in your debt. It's not right for us to ask even more of you."

"I'm not giving up now." Pippa's eyes burned with determination. "I promised to save Chevalia and I will!"

"Stardust," said the queen, "make your friend see that it's too dangerous."

Stardust tossed her head. "No, Mom. Pippa is right. We can't give up now, not when we're so close to saving Chevalia."

The queen sighed in acceptance.

Reaching out, she nuzzled Stardust and Pippa closer and hugged them tight.

"Stardust, you're the bravest foal I know. And you, Pippa, are the most courageous girl."

Pippa blushed.

"You haven't met any other girls," she said modestly.

"I don't have to," the queen said with a smile. "So where will your search take you today?"

"The Volcano," Pippa said immediately. "That's where the hooded pony ran to with the horseshoes we found yesterday, which suggests the eighth one is hidden there as well."

Pippa knew that if she said it was Divine who had stolen the horseshoes, the queen wouldn't believe her. Pippa would have to prove it.

"Then you know your path," said the queen. "Good luck, Pippa. Good luck, Stardust. Be safe."

Chapter 2

Pippa rode Stardust out of the castle and over the drawbridge, toward the base of the Volcano. As they began climbing the rugged foothills, the Volcano towered above them, its fiery top illuminating the sky. Now and then a puff of smoke rose in the air, spilling red cinders that drifted over the Cloud Forest and onto the lower slopes.

"It's getting hotter the closer we get

to the Volcano," Stardust said, stopping to catch her breath.

"I'll walk," Pippa said, starting to slide from Stardust's back.

"No," the princess pony said quickly. "I like it when you ride on me. It feels right."

She shied, narrowly avoiding a cloud of sparks as they shot to the ground.

"Even the Volcano feels angry. Maybe this really is the end for Chevalia."

"Never," Pippa said forcefully.

They continued in silence and soon they entered the mysterious Cloud Forest, home to the secretive unicorns. The forest felt cool and fresh. Pippa loved the way the sunlight filtered through the ancient trees, dotting the path with golden puddles of light. Stardust slowed down, weaving a careful path through the forest to avoid the enormous vines that trailed from branches like long snakes. They were over halfway through the forest when the hairs on Pippa's neck rose and her arms tingled with goosebumps. Convinced she was being watched, she looked around.

"What's wrong?" asked Stardust.

The forest around them was silent and still. As they stared into the cloudy gloom suddenly something jumped from a tree and stood on the path ahead. Stardust flinched then burst out laughing.

"Misty!" she cried.

Pippa appreciated once more just

how similar Misty was to Stardust. The unicorn was almost identical to her friend, from the tilt of her head to the tip of her snow-white tail. The only differences were the pretty golden horn on the top of Misty's head and their size—Misty was the size of a large dog.

"Hello!" Misty's musical voice bubbled with excitement. "Is it time already? Have you come to get us for the Midsummer Concert?"

Stardust shook her head sadly.

"I'm sorry, Misty, but there might not be a concert now. One of the horseshoes is still missing."

"No!" Misty gasped. "But it's Midsummer Day."

"That's why we're here. We're on our way to the Volcano—we think the horseshoe could be hidden there," Pippa said.

They quickly told Misty everything that had happened since the unicorns had helped them retrieve a missing horseshoe from the Cloud Forest.

"That's awful." Misty's eyes were wide with alarm. "I'm coming with you."

"It might be dangerous," Stardust warned her.

"It'll be more dangerous if the horse-shoe isn't found," Misty answered.

The trio set off at a brisk trot. It was fun having Misty with them. She knew the Cloud Forest like the back of her hoof and showed them a much quicker route through it. But it was still a long way.

Finally, they emerged from the treeline at the base of the Volcano and continued up its blackened slopes. The ground grew hotter, and Stardust and Misty hopped from hoof to hoof, trying to avoid stepping on the lumps of hot volcanic rock. The path twisted and turned and, as they trotted around a corner, Stardust came to an abrupt halt. Misty almost ran into her and only just stopped in time. A giant river of lava blocked the path. Pippa turned her face away from the fiery heat rising from the bubbling red liquid.

"That was close," Stardust said, carefully stepping backward. "We'll have to find another way around."

Pippa considered the bubbling lava, which stretched as far as she could see in both directions.

"That could take ages," she said. "It would be much quicker to cross it."

Her brain whirred with images as she tried to work out a solution. Luckily one came to her.

"Misty, could you freeze the lava with your magical horn?"

"I've never frozen something so hot before," Misty said doubtfully. "But I'll try."

Bravely, she stepped right up to the edge of the flowing lava.

"Careful," Pippa warned as a shower of sparks cascaded to the ground.

Misty lowered her head until the tip of her horn touched the lava. She winced then backed away.

"It's not working," she said sadly. "It's too hot and it burned me. Plus, I can sense that the lava has a magic of its

own. My magic would never be strong enough to freeze it."

As if the lava river was aware of its audience, it began to hiss. Bubbles rose to the surface, rapidly growing to the size of balloons before popping. They smelled of rotten eggs.

Stardust wrinkled her nose.

"Phooey! That's disgusting."

"We're going to have to jump it," Pippa said at last.

"I can't! It's too wide," Stardust squeaked.

"But there isn't another way around."

Stardust edged away from the hissing lava.

"'I'm sorry, Pippa, but I can't. It's much too wide."

"I bet you could if you tried. You jumped much farther than this yesterday when the wild ponies taught you how to free-trot."

Stardust stared at the lava rolling across their path. "Did I?" she said in a small voice.

"Yes, you did," Pippa said encouragingly, stroking her mane.

"But I'm scared!"

"I know," said Pippa. "But I've been scared so many times during our adventures, and I always knew you'd help me. Why don't we practice first? My mom always says *practice makes perfect*. Look— there are lots of boulders to jump over in preparation."

"All right," Stardust said finally.

Turning away from the lava, she began to hop over boulders, starting with the smaller ones. Each time she cleared one, Pippa cheered loudly. Misty joined in, stomping her hooves excitedly. Stardust's confidence grew, until soon she was jumping large boulders, clearing them with ease.

"Faster!" urged Misty. "The faster you run at the jump, the easier it is. Watch me."

Misty galloped toward a boulder almost twice her height. She cleared it with a triumphant flick of her hind hooves. Stardust stared in amazement. Singling out a boulder almost three times her height, she pawed at the ground then took off at a gallop.

"Brilliant!" Pippa shouted, as Stardust cleared the boulder with half a yard to spare.

Stardust pulled up, her sides heaving as she struggled to catch her breath.

"I'm ready," she said when she was breathing normally again.

A shiver of fear ran down Pippa's spine. Now that the moment had come to jump the lava river, *she* didn't want to do it.

Swallowing back her panic, she said, "Let's do it for Chevalia!"

Stardust turned away from the lava river. She went so far away from it that for a second Pippa wondered if she was running away. Then she turned on her hind hooves. Taking a deep breath, she put her head down and galloped toward the lava. A stride's length away she jumped, muscles bunching as she launched herself skyward. Pippa's face and arms glowed in the fiery heat beneath her. She held her breath, hardly daring to look down. Stardust hit the ground with a thump and galloped

several strides before she was able to pull up.

"We did it," she gasped.

"*You* did it," Pippa corrected her.

"We!" Stardust shouted to make her voice heard over Misty's triumphant cheers. "That was teamwork. I could never have done it without your help."

"We help each other all the time," said Pippa.

"I know," Stardust said happily. "It's what best friends do."

"It's my turn now," called Misty.

Stardust turned to watch the little unicorn run at the lava. Her golden horn bobbed up and down as she ran toward the molten river. There was a determined sparkle in her eye as she took off. She cleared the lava in one giant leap and her smile was brighter than the morning sun as she landed gracefully.

Pippa and Stardust cheered, but there was no time to rest. The three friends continued steadily up the Volcano.

"How much farther?" Stardust asked.

"We're nearly there," said Misty.

As the climb became steeper, Stardust and Misty fell silent, saving their energy for the ascent. Sweat trickled from Pippa's scalp and ran down her forehead into her eyes. Her wavy hair felt limp, like seaweed stranded on the beach. She pushed the hair from her face. What would they find at the top of the Volcano? With the hungry, red flames belching skyward, it was hard to imagine anything existing up there at all. The path continued to wind until, rounding another bend, Stardust stopped sharply.

"What's that?"

"It's a castle!" Pippa said, her heart pounding against her ribs.

Ahead of them was the biggest castle she'd ever seen, built into the face of the Volcano. Its towers loomed above them, with their tall, slit windows staring out like many eyes. Ebony towers spiked upward from behind a solid jet wall. A massive drawbridge was drawn up, preventing intruders from crossing a moat of bubbling orange-red lava and reaching an enormous, coal-colored door.

The whole place had a forbidding look. Even the craggy stone walls seemed to shout, "*Go away!*"

Stardust gave a huge, sad sigh.

"I don't believe it. We've come all this way and now we can't get in."

Chapter 3

Pippa squinted, scanning the Volcano Castle for a way in. She spotted guard ponies staring down over the walls.

"Look," she said, pointing. "The guards have seen us. They're lowering the drawbridge."

Two stern-faced Night Mares, wearing black sashes encrusted with diamonds, were letting the drawbridge down.

"Why would they do that right away,"

Pippa asked, "unless they're expecting us?"

"You mean it could be a trap?" Stardust asked, her voice squeaky with fear.

"Maybe—perhaps Divine guessed that we'd come after her."

"We don't have to go in," Misty said, taking dainty steps backward.

"We do," said Pippa. "It's our best chance of finding the last horseshoe."

As the drawbridge lowered over the moat, the guard ponies motioned for them to cross it and come up. Stardust stepped forward, and, after a hoof beat's hesitation, Misty followed. The flapping of wings made Pippa look up.

Something soared overhead and was gone in a flash. She gazed at the sky but there was nothing there. She gripped onto Stardust's mane as the princess pony trotted across the rattling drawbridge.

"Welcome, strangers," neighed the guards.

"Hello," Stardust whinnied back. "Please, can we come in?"

The Night Mares exchanged a grin.

"Of course," said the taller one. "It's a pleasure to have you here. It's not often that we get to welcome visitors."

Pippa could feel Stardust shaking beneath her. Taking a deep breath to steady her own trembling hand, she patted Stardust's neck. Bravely Stardust stepped up into the castle, which appeared to be the home of the Night Mares. Having passed through the enormous door, they found themselves in a courtyard.

"It's just like the one back home, only there's no Whispering Wall," exclaimed Stardust.

"There's no wall at all," said Pippa.

The courtyard stretched away and opened out into a long, stone balcony that overhung a huge pool of bubbling lava. Tearing her eyes away from the smoldering pool, Pippa stared upward and saw the blue sky dotted with fluffy, white clouds.

"This must be the heart of the Volcano," she whispered.

Her eyes widened as she took in their surroundings. The lava pool was indeed the very center of the Volcano, with a whole world carved into the rock around it. Pippa saw caves of all sizes linked by walkways of black stone. There were spires decorated with scary stone pony gargoyles that spat rivers of molten lava into the pit below. There were graceful arches and stone pillars all elaborately carved with the heads of ponies. The lava pool lit the caves, towers, and arches with a soft red glow. Pippa shivered despite the heat.

"Look how busy everyone is," Misty said in wonder.

Ponies bustled about, nodding to each other as they hurried past. Pippa gripped Stardust's mane as two familiar ponies trotted by.

"Look!" she gasped. "That's Nightshade and Eclipse."

"Hey, you!" Stardust shouted. "You stole our first horseshoe."

Several ponies stopped and stared, but Stardust ignored them and kept shouting until Nightshade turned around. She trotted over, closely followed by Eclipse.

"We did not," she said angrily. "The Mistress gave us that horseshoe. She said it belonged to her and that we must hide it for a game."

"That's not true," Stardust said, shaking her head. "The Mistress stole all eight horseshoes from the Royal Family. She took them from our ancient Whispering Wall, where they've hung for centuries."

"Are you sure?" asked Eclipse. "But the Mistress is our loyal protector— she wouldn't steal anything."

"The horseshoes belong here, where they were made," Nightshade argued.

"They were made here," agreed Stardust, "but they truly belong on the Whispering Wall. It's written in the

ancient scrolls. If you don't believe me then check."

"Ancient scrolls? I've never heard of any scrolls," Nightshade said. "And you shouldn't go around shouting at ponies that they're thieves," she added angrily. "Is that how they teach Royal Ponies to behave at Stableside?"

Pippa could see that the argument was going nowhere and that Nightshade was getting angry.

"Stardust didn't mean to call you a thief," Pippa said apologetically. "We're just really worried about the horseshoes—the last one must be found before the end of the day. We didn't know anyone actually lived inside the Volcano. It's amazing here—I'd love to look around."

Pippa smiled shyly and Nightshade smiled right back.

"Thank you. I think it's beautiful, but our home isn't to everyone's taste. I could show you around if you like?"

Pippa's face lit up.

"Yes, please!"

Eclipse stepped forward, staring at Pippa through her long, shaggy mane.

"You're from Stableside, aren't you? Those ponies are so stuck-up. They think they're the only ones with a proper castle. You wait till you see what we have here. Our castle is the best! It doesn't get much grander or older. This castle was here long before Stableside. It's the very heart of Chevalia."

"Really?" Pippa frowned. "So why would you want to destroy the island?"

Eclipse looked at Nightshade, who shrugged.

"What are you talking about?"

"The horseshoe that you were hiding for a game," Pippa said carefully, "is definitely one of the eight magical horseshoes that should hang on the ancient Whispering Wall. The scientist-magician Nightingale wrote in her scrolls that Chevalia can only survive if the horseshoes' magic— and the love they capture from pony and horse lovers around the world— is renewed by the rays of the sun every Midsummer."

Eclipse's eyes widened in alarm.

"What?" she whispered. "Is that really true?"

Pippa nodded.

"Then the Mistress has misled us." Nightshade looked ready to burst into tears. "She told us that the horseshoes were symbols of power and that by hiding them, Chevalia would return to its former glory, where the Volcano was the heart of the island and every pony was equal."

"Every pony should be equal," Pippa agreed, "but stealing the horseshoes isn't going to help. If you read the ancient scrolls, you'll realize that before Night-ingale created the horseshoes, the island was just a small lump of volcanic rock—there was no former glory!"

"We must find the eighth missing horseshoe," Stardust said urgently. "We think it's here somewhere but we don't know where to look."

"We'll help," Nightshade said immediately.

Eclipse jumped up and when she spoke her voice was high with excitement.

"I think I know where it is. Nightingale had a laboratory hidden deep in the Volcano. The Mistress spends all her time there—she locked herself inside it all last night. I bet that's where she's hidden the last horseshoe. Follow me and I'll show you."

Eclipse took off at a smart trot. In single file, Nightshade, Stardust, and Misty hurried after her along several winding stone walkways and tunnels. The tunnels led to one side of the Volcano's inner rim and a series of caves.

"Nightingale's laboratory is in the last cave," Eclipse said, panting slightly as she walked around the puddles of lava and the black boulders littering the ground.

Eventually they came to an archway with a stone door and an iron latch. Eclipse flipped the latch up and pushed.

The door opened with a groan. In silence everyone walked inside, and Pippa dismounted from Stardust. Long benches covered with glass beakers that were coated with dust lined the middle of the cave. There were test tubes everywhere, filled with brightly colored liquids. Pippa's throat tightened at the acid smell of chemicals. A huge cream scroll tied with a dark pink ribbon lay on top of a wooden desk. Pippa's eyes were drawn to it. Was that the original ancient scroll or just a copy? Next to it, in a frame made from volcanic rock, was a picture of a stocky pony with bulging eyes.

"Divine?" Stardust asked, stepping forward.

"No, it's Nightingale," Nightshade corrected her. "The Mistress is a direct descendant of Nightingale. But, yes, they're very similar."

There were more portraits of Night-ingale on the walls, hanging in ornate

gold frames. The last picture had a modern frame and was of a smaller pony with eyes that protruded even more.

"That's Divine," Pippa exclaimed, pointing. Her voice rose suddenly. "And hanging above the picture is the last horseshoe!"

"Yes it is."

The voice that came from the doorway sent shivers racing along Pippa's spine. It was Baroness Divine.

"I've been expecting you." Divine smiled evilly. Throwing back her head, she laughed triumphantly, then she shouted, "Guards, seize them!"

Chapter 4

A group of Night Mares, wearing the guards' uniform of diamond-encrusted black sashes, charged into the laboratory and surrounded Pippa, Stardust, and Misty. They marched them outside and into a long, dark tunnel lit by flickering torches. As the tunnel twisted and turned it kept splitting into more passages.

"Left, right, right, left, left, left,"

Pippa murmured to herself as she tried to memorize the route they were taking.

They were traveling downhill and, after entering a very narrow tunnel, they finally arrived at their destination.

"The dungeons," Stardust neighed, her breath catching.

The guards roughly nudged the trio into the same cell. The door clanged shut and the key scraped in the lock.

Divine's hoof steps rang out mockingly as she started to trot away.

"You've failed." Divine laughed.

"Wait!" cried Pippa. "Why are you doing this to us?"

Divine turned around to face them. Stopping, she said, "Nightingale may be

my distant ancestor, but she was a fool.
When she found magical gold in the
Volcano she fashioned it into two sets
of symbolic horseshoes, one set each
for the king and queen of the new
island of Chevalia that the horseshoes
went on to create. The island was a
place where all ponies could be equal.
But how could that ever be when
Nightingale had decreed that there would
be a king and queen? Far better, I say, that
the island remains a volcanic rock, led by
only one pony. My plan is to destroy the
last golden horseshoe so that Chevalia
will return to what it was—a simple
place with no Royal Court or princess
ponies. There will be just one leader. Me.
I shall rule the new volcanic island."

Stardust let out a loud sob then bravely swallowed to stop any more from escaping.

"How are you going to destroy the horseshoe?" asked Pippa. Her heart hammered in her chest as she tried to buy some time.

Divine's eyes glowed in the torchlight.

"I plan to throw it into the heart of the Volcano, where the hot lava will melt it."

"Won't that be dangerous?" Pippa asked. "What about the magic locked inside the horseshoe?"

"Enough!" roared Divine. "My plan is nearly complete. I don't have time to waste talking to a silly little girl."

The Baroness walked away, the

guards following, their hooves echoing on the rough floor.

Stardust huddled in the corner of the cell and began to cry. Pippa wrapped her arms around her friend's neck. She buried her face in Stardust's silky mane, breathing in her sweet pony smell.

"Don't cry," she said gently. "It's not over yet."

"But it is," Stardust wept. "How can we ever escape from here? Divine will destroy the eighth horseshoe and Chevalia will disappear. I'm never going to see my family again." Her voice rose to a wail.

Pippa continued to hug her. She

wanted to say something wise and comforting but the words wouldn't come. At last she pulled away from Stardust to examine the dungeon bars. They ran from floor to ceiling and were as solid as a mountain. They didn't even rattle when Pippa tried to shake them.

"We're truly stuck," she said as Misty came to stand beside her. "Unless . . ." An idea popped into Pippa's head. With mounting excitement she said, "Misty, could you use your unicorn magic to freeze the bars?'"

Misty stared at her for a moment, then a slow smile spread over her face. As Stardust realized what Pippa intended, she stood beside her.

"I think so," said Misty.

As the unicorn bent her head forward, Pippa was amazed by how delicate her spiraled horn looked against the thick prison bar. Could something so tiny and beautiful overpower the iron's strength?

"Yes," Pippa said softly.

She clenched her hands into fists. It was like good and evil. Good always won in the end if people had the courage to stand together and fight the bad.

A cracking noise echoed around the prison cell as, slowly, the bars began to freeze. Pippa could feel the cold radiating from them.

"It's your turn now, Stardust," said Pippa. "Can you kick the bars out?"

Stardust shook back her long, white

mane. There was a look of determination in her brown eyes.

"Easy!" she said.

Turning her back on the bars, Stardust lashed out with her hind hooves
and there was an earsplitting crack.
Stardust kicked again and again. Suddenly the bars fell to the floor.

"Hooray!" cheered Pippa.

She scrambled up on Stardust's back.

"Now we go after Divine."

At a fast trot, Stardust and Misty fled the dungeon into the dark tunnel. Many of the flickering torches had been snuffed out. Pippa squinted as they flew along, but the passageway didn't look familiar.

"Left," she said uncertainly as they reached the first branch of the underground labyrinth.

Pippa clung onto Stardust's back, ducking her head in the places where the ceiling was low. Stardust's and Misty's breathing came in noisy rasps. They continued for a while, until they reached a crossroad of four paths. Pippa hesitated.

"Which way?" Stardust asked, pulling up.

Fear gripped Pippa's insides. She didn't remember this part of the tunnel at all. There was a buzzing noise in her ears. Pippa shook her head in irritation.

"Watch out!" cried a tiny voice. "It's meee. Your good friend Zzzimb."

"Zimb!" Pippa's spirits soared as her horsefly friend flew in front of her face and landed on her nose. Pippa giggled and crossed her eyes as she tried to focus on him.

Zimb chuckled too, then flew away to perch on Stardust's ear.

"A little losssssst, are we? Let Zzzimb help."

There was a faint buzz and suddenly

the tunnel glowed with a thousand pinpricks of light.

"Fireflies!" Pippa said, staring around in delight.

"Weee ssssaw you enter the Volcano," said Zimb. "No Royal Pony has ever ventured here before. Weee guesssssed you might need help."

"Thank you," said Stardust.

Quickly Pippa, Stardust, and Misty told Zimb why they were in the Volcano.

"Baronesssss Divine hassss assembled everyone in the castle courtyard," said Zimb. "Weeee sssssaw her on our way in. Hurry!"

Stardust and Misty galloped through the tunnels, led by Zimb and the light of the fireflies showing them where to go. Together they burst into the castle courtyard. As Stardust pulled up, Pippa gasped.

"Wow!" she exclaimed, her eyes staring at the huge crowd of Night Mares assembled in front of Divine.

No one noticed Pippa, Stardust, Misty, Zimb, and the fireflies join the back of the crowd. All eyes were on Divine, who stood on a platform of black rock as she addressed the crowd. Crowning her head was the eighth golden horseshoe, glinting in the fierce light of the Volcano.

"The time has come. This Midsummer Day will go down in our history, for today marks the start of a wonderful new era for the ponies of the Volcano. We are gathered here to witness the end of the Royal Realm. Nightingale was wrong to have meddled with magic. She never should have created Chevalia and allowed ponies from the human world to come here. I will reverse her mistake. By throwing this horseshoe into the lava,

our volcanic island will return to the way it was. Down with Chevalia! Long live Volcanica!"

A loud cheer resounded from the Night Mares and they stomped their hooves with approval.

Out of the corner of her eye, Pippa saw Nightshade and Eclipse huddled together. Their eyes were huge with worry and they shook their heads in disbelief.

"Only they know the truth," Pippa said softly. "If Divine destroys that horseshoe, she'll destroy the whole island."

Chapter 5

The cheers rose to a crescendo, and with it the courtyard darkened. Pippa stared up. What was the dark shape that was spreading closer, like spilled ink? The Night Mares fell silent. A soft whooshing noise filled the air. It reminded Pippa of wings.

"Cloud!" she exclaimed as the silver-gray princess pony led a flock of flying ponies into the courtyard.

"Mom, Dad! Crystal, Cinders . . ." Stardust's voice was soft with wonder as the entire Royal Court flew into sight and hovered above them.

"I saw you enter the Volcano," said Cloud. "I thought you'd probably need some help."

"And I think I saw you!" Pippa exclaimed, thinking of when they stepped into the Volcano Castle and she'd noticed something in the sky.

Cloud swooped down and rubbed her nose first against Stardust's and then Misty's nose. There was a loud crack and a bright flash of light as they both sprouted wings. Pippa adjusted her position on Stardust's back around the princess pony's new wings.

"You dare to invade my castle?" Divine demanded, her eyes rolling wildly. "What's the meaning of this?"

"We've come to save Chevalia, for the good of all the ponies who live here," Cloud replied.

"Too late!" shrieked Divine.

She tossed her head and the golden horseshoe spun into the air. It flew over the Volcano, spinning in the wind. Then it fell toward the fiery pit of the Volcano.

Pippa shouted to Stardust, "Get it!"

Stardust flew down, her mane and tail flying behind her straighter than arrows. Pippa hung on tightly, gritting her teeth as the hot volcanic air washed over them. Far below she could see the lava glimmering red. The horse-shoe spun toward it, flashing in the fiery light.

Stardust flew even faster. Pippa could feel the pony's muscles straining as she dived toward the molten heart of the Volcano far below. Burying her left hand in Stardust's mane to anchor herself, she reached out for the spin-ning horseshoe. Her fingers touched it, but then the horseshoe spun away. Stardust flew faster still. Pippa reached out again. She was so close. Her wavy hair streamed out behind her and the wind rushed in her ears. Her fingers ached as they reached for the horse-shoe and, this time, she caught it. The horseshoe tingled in her hand as magic

coursed through her fingertips. It filled her with warmth, excitement, and hope.

"We did it!" she shouted.

Stardust whinnied with delight and, turning around, she soared upward. She flew over the courtyard and circled it in a lap of victory. Pippa sat tall on

her back, proudly holding the horseshoe in the air for everyone to see.

"Stupid fools! You've ruined everything," Divine shrieked with rage.

"No," shouted Stardust. "*You* would
have ruined everything, but now
Chevalia is safe for us all to live in and
enjoy again."

"She's right," Nightshade and Eclipse
called out. "The Mistress wanted the
island for herself. She doesn't care what
happens to us."

The Royal Ponies flying overhead
cheered wildly, but the Volcano ponies
looked doubtfully between Divine and
Stardust, unsure who to believe.

"Nightingale created the horseshoes and Chevalia for everyone," said

Nightshade. "Why would Divine want to destroy them unless it was for her own gain?"

It was as if the Night Mares had suddenly woken up. Their faces cleared as they understood the truth, and they burst into noisy cheers.

"To Chevalia!"

The applause and cheering lasted for a while. As the noise finally died away, Stardust spoke.

"We haven't succeeded yet. For Chevalia to remain the beautiful place it is, we have to hang this horseshoe on the ancient Whispering Wall by sundown."

Queen Moonshine flew over the center of the courtyard.

"Go quickly, my foal—time is running out. Then tonight we will celebrate, first with a Royal Concert with our new friends the unicorns, then with the Midsummer Ball. Everyone is invited—you are all my guests. From this day forth the Royal Ponies and the Volcano ponies will be better friends. The island of Chevalia belongs to us all."

"Never!" shrieked Divine. "I will never allow it."

The guards surrounded Divine, but she was too quick. Leaping in the air, she threw herself at Queen Moonshine. The queen backed away in alarm, flapping her pale gold wings, but not before Divine had rubbed noses with her.

There was a brilliant flash of light and a crack split the air as the Baroness sprouted her own wings. Whinnying in triumph, Divine flew away.

"Stop her," shouted the guards.

Ponies bolted in all directions, until the queen called them to attention.

"Don't fear Divine. It's unlikely that

she'll show her face around here again. But if she does, we'll be ready for her. If all of us stand together, we can stop her from carrying out any more evil plans."

Pippa leaned forward and spoke into her friend's ear.

"Stardust, we have to go."

"I know," said Stardust. "Hold on tight, Pippa."

The princess pony's white wings flapped gracefully as she rose up and out of the Volcano and headed for home.

Chapter 6

With the sun setting behind her, Stardust flew straight to Stableside Castle. Pippa urged her to fly faster as the sinking sun fell toward the horizon. As Stableside came into view, the sun was merely a golden sliver above the darkening sea. With a burst of energy, Stardust flew over the castle walls and landed in the Royal Courtyard. The moment her hooves touched the ground, her wings disappeared. Pippa had to hold on tightly.

"There's not much time left," Stardust said as she approached the ancient Whispering Wall.

Pippa heard the rush of wings as the entire Royal Court returned behind them. All but Cloud landed in the courtyard—she remained above the ground, keeping her hooves tucked up beneath her.

The last rays of the sun lit the seven golden horseshoes on the wall. The magic crackled as it renewed itself, but Pippa could see the bare patch of wall where the eighth horseshoe needed to be placed.

As Stardust came next to the wall,

Pippa stood up on her back. A smile tugged at her lips as she remembered how scared she'd been the very first time she'd stood on Stardust. That had been to rescue the first golden horseshoe. She'd never completely got rid of her fear of heights but she'd come a long way to manage it. Proudly Pippa reached up and hung the golden horseshoe back where it belonged.

A sunray slanted toward it and, reaching down, kissed the horseshoe with its buttermilk glow. There was a moment of complete silence, then the Whispering Wall seemed to let out an electric sizzle. Suddenly it was as if someone had lit a thousand sparklers. The horseshoes glittered brighter than

the noonday sun as their energy was fully renewed.

A huge cheer rose into the air, along with cries of "Chevalia forever!"

Pippa slid from Stardust's back and threw her arms around her friend's neck.

"We did it," she sobbed. Happiness

filled her like a mountain stream. "We found all the missing horseshoes. We saved Chevalia."

Stardust nuzzled Pippa's hair.

"Thank you, Pippa," she neighed. "And thank you for being my best friend."

As the very last ray of sunlight disappeared, a warm, amber light bathed the whole island. The energized horseshoes were charging the island's magic for another year. Stardust stood very still, drinking it in. All of a sudden, for Pippa, time froze. The courtyard became sketchy like a shadow, and through it she could see her family on the beach in the horseshoe-shaped cove. Her mother, brother, and sister were as still as statues, sitting with a picnic half laid out before them. A wave of longing swept over Pippa. She missed her family so much it hurt.

The light disappeared, leaving Stardust and Pippa in the darkness. Time moved on again.

"I love Chevalia," Pippa said softly, "but I love my own home too. It's time I returned to my family."

"Of course," said Stardust. "You can't leave just yet, though."

Pippa raised an eyebrow, making Stardust giggle.

"You can't miss the Royal Concert or the Midsummer Ball."

☆

There was so little time to prepare for the concert that everyone pitched in and helped. Pippa smiled as Queen Moonshine rushed past her with a huge bunch of wildflowers for King Firestar to hang around the Royal Court.

Just as the last garland was put in place, the unicorns arrived from the Cloud Forest. They were greeted by court advisers who'd hurriedly changed into their best sashes and who ushered all the guests to the courtyard.

The opening bars of music soared in the air and Pippa's heart flew with it as she was carried away by the exquisite voices. Honey's coat looked pale in the moonlight as her duet approached. She needn't have worried. She sang beautifully, her confidence boosted by her unicorn twin and singing partner, Goldie. Afterward Stardust whispered to Pippa that the concert was the best one Chevalia had ever held. Queen Moonshine thought so too.

"Much good has come from these troubled times. The ponies and unicorns who live here on Chevalia need not fear each other anymore. We will work and play together for the good of the island and all ponykind."

"What, even the Night Mares?" called a pony who hadn't flown to the Volcano with the Royal Family.

"Especially the *Volcano ponies*," Queen Moonshine answered. "They're no different than us."

The courtyard was full of nervous neighs, but when the Volcano ponies arrived for the ball, shyly shuffling their hooves, every single pony welcomed them warmly.

Riding on Stardust's back as they danced with Prince Jet and Prince Storm, Pippa was bursting with happiness.

"Ouch!" Stardust squeaked, as Jet stepped on her hoof again.

"Sorry." Jet blushed. "Dancing's not really my thing."

"Look at Crystal and Trojan." Honey giggled, pointing to the other side of the room with a sparkly hoof.

Crystal and Trojan, the farm pony from the Grasslands, were dancing together, nuzzling as they swayed to the music.

"And there's Blossom," Stardust said, her eyes wide with surprise. "Who'd have thought my 'clumsy' friend would be so good at dancing?!"

"It just shows you don't know what you're good at until you try different things," Pippa said, remembering all the new things she'd tried and achieved in the last week.

There was a huge banquet at the ball. Pippa realized how hungry she was as she and Stardust ate from the flower-decorated troughs. Stardust enjoyed honey-dipped carrots

and roasted oats while Pippa polished off a glass of lemonade and a plate of fish and fries prepared especially for her.

Soon the wonderful Midsummer evening was drawing to a close. As the ponies began to drift back to their stables, Princess Cloud flew overhead.

"It's time, Pippa. I'm here to take you home."

Stardust's eyes filled with tears.

"I can hardly bear to let you go," she whinnied.

Cloud looked at her youngest sister.

"Would you like to come with us and fly your friend home?" she asked.

"Yes," Stardust said immediately. "I'd love that."

Cloud flew over to rub Stardust's nose and right away she grew a huge pair of feathery, white wings. Pippa neatly jumped onto her back amid cries of farewell from her new friends.

Queen Moonshine's voice rose above them all.

"Good-bye, Pippa MacDonald, friend of Chevalia. You're always welcome here. Come back and see us soon."

Pippa choked back her tears.

"I will," she said, waving. "Bye, Honey. Bye, Goldie. Bye, Blossom and Misty, Comet, Jet, Crystal, Storm, King Fire-star, Peggy, and good-bye, Cinders."

With a dip of their wings, Stardust

and Cloud rose into the moonlit sky and up over the glass-like sea.

"Wait," Pippa cried, seeing two huge horselike forms emerging from the water. "It's Triton and Rosella!"

The giant seahorses bowed their heads as Stardust hovered above them.

"Pippa, lover of ponies, thank you for saving our island," they yelled.

"Thank you for helping me," Pippa yelled back.

A warm glow filled Pippa as Stardust sped away. She was glad she'd seen her seahorse friends one last time. It was with them that the entire adventure on Chevalia had started.

Stardust and Cloud flew side by side in silence. Gradually the dark night gave way to the rosy light of dawn and the sky brightened, until it was blue in the midday sun.

Cloud and Stardust both slowed, their huge wings straining with effort.

"Can you feel it?" asked Cloud. "We've left the magic time bubble behind. You're nearly home, Pippa."

Pippa wrapped her arms around Stardust's soft neck.

"Best friend," she whispered, "I'm going to miss you."

"I'll miss you too," Stardust said, her voice full of tears. "But remember— it's not good-bye. We'll meet again. I know it."

"Me too," said Pippa.

They were hovering just above the sand by the horseshoe-shaped cove. Pippa hugged Stardust one last time and, as she did so, Stardust pressed something cold into Pippa's hand.

"To remember me by," she said softly.

Then Pippa slid from Stardust's back and dropped to the soft sand. The whir of wings overhead faded and, as Pippa stared into the bright blue sky, Cloud and Stardust vanished.

The beach was quiet except for the soft hiss of the sea as it lapped against the shore. Pippa rubbed her eyes.

Suddenly it was hard to imagine she'd been anywhere at all. Had she fallen asleep and had the most amazing dream? Her hand tightened around something solid. She unclenched her fingers and in her palm was Stardust's sparkly pink tiara. Pippa stared at it for a few seconds then carefully slid it into the pocket of her shorts. As she did so, she realized she was back in her own clothes.

"Pippa!"

Mom was calling.

Pippa raced up the beach. Mom was just putting up a parasol over a blanket that was spread with an amazing picnic. The Midsummer Ball now seemed a lifetime ago and she was ravenously hungry. Sitting down between her sister, Miranda, and her brother, Jack, she reached for a sandwich.

"This is going to be the best vacation ever," Pippa declared.

Mom smiled as she handed out cups of juice.

"And that's even before I've told you about my final surprise."

Pippa hurriedly swallowed a mouthful of sandwich.

"What surprise?" she asked.

"I know how much you like ponies—"

"*Love* ponies," Pippa corrected her.

Mom smiled. "Just down the lane from the vacation cottage there's a riding school, and guess what? I've arranged for you to have riding lessons.

Wouldn't you love to learn to ride a pony?"

Pippa was speechless for a moment. Then she jumped up and hugged her mom so hard that she nearly dropped her drink.

"Thanks, Mom. It's a dream come true!"

Chevalia Now!

EXCLUSIVE INTERVIEW WITH PIPPA AND PRINCESS STARDUST

by Tulip Inkhoof

1

While Chevalia was celebrating the return of the eight magical horseshoes and enjoying the festivities, this dedicated reporter interviewed Princess Stardust and Pippa MacDonald in between the Royal Concert and the Midsummer Ball. ✧ ✧ ✧

☆ **TI (Tulip Inkhoof):** Well, you two are certainly the toast of the party. How does it feel to have saved Chevalia?

☆ **S (Princess Stardust):** It feels incredible!

☆ **P (Pippa):** It does feel great but, Stardust, let's not forget that saving the horseshoes was a team effort. We couldn't have done it by ourselves.

☆ **S:** You're right, Pippa—the entire island came together to help.

☆ **TI:** Yes, and even the Night Mares are here at the castle for the ball?

☆ **S:** You mean the Volcano ponies, don't you? We used to call them Night Mares but that was an unfair name— we never took the time to get to know them. The Volcano ponies are the original inhabitants of Chevalia, and our very special friends.

☆ **P:** That's very grown-up of you, Stardust. I think you've learned a lot this week.

☆ **TI:** My word, have you only been on Chevalia for a week, Pippa?

☆ **P:** Yes, I can't believe it either!

☆ **S:** As soon as I saw this real, live girl on the beach that first morning,  I just knew she'd come to save the island. What I didn't know was that she'd become my best friend too!

☆ **P:** I'm going to miss you so much, Stardust.

☆ **S:** Do you really have to go home to the human world? Can't you stay on Chevalia?

☆ **P:** It's so tempting, but I love my family and, even though they're not missing me because of the time bubble, the truth is that I miss them.

☆ **S:** I understand—I'd miss my family too.

☆ **TI:** What will you do back in the human world, Pippa? It's such a mystery to us Chevalia ponies.

☆ **P:** Well, we'll still be on vacation when I return, which I'm really looking forward to, and soon after that it's back to school.

☆ **S:** Won't you miss the excitement of Chevalia?

☆ **P:** Of course I will, but Chevalia will always be in my heart and in my memories. Besides, everything can be an adventure.

☆ **S:** That's so true—and I hope I have an adventure every single day!

☆ **TI:** Then that will give me a lot to report on!

And with that, Stardust tugged Pippa onto the dance floor for the first dance of the Midsummer Ball, leaving this young reporter to reflect on the incredibly eventful week. This was a week in which our beautiful island was saved and the Royal Ponies made friends with the once mysterious, and long misunderstood, Volcano ponies.

☆ Chevalia Now, Chevalia Forever! ☆

Queen Moonshine and **King Firestar**
invite all the ponies on Chevalia
to the **Midsummer Ball**
at Stableside Castle

A Midsummer celebration with dancing
and a delicious banquet

Please welcome the Volcano ponies
as they make their Castle debut

Dress code: wear your best sashes and sparkliest tiaras!

Dear Ponies of Chevalia,

I'm writing this letter on the big wooden table in our vacation cottage, and I plan to give it to Triton and Rosella to deliver before we drive back to Burlington Terrace.

It's hard to believe I've been back with my family for a whole week. In my heart it feels like I haven't left Chevalia at all.

As soon as Stardust and Cloud dropped me off at the beach, I heard Mom calling me for lunch. We had a delicious picnic on the sand with my sister, Miranda, and my little brother, Jack. While we were eating,

I had the most wonderful surprise—Mom told me she was going to treat me to riding lessons! Every day for the past week, I had lessons with an amazing pony called Snowdrop—the pony from my dreams!

Mrs. Woods, the lady who runs the riding school, encouraged us to learn eventing. Together Snowdrop and I tried dressage, cross-country, and showjumping. Snowdrop and I were such a perfect match that Mrs. Woods said I should return to train with Snowdrop during my next school vacation. I do hope Mom agrees! Perhaps I could visit Chevalia too? Please cross your hooves for me!

Now it's time to return to our house, to school, and to normal life . . . I miss you all so much, especially Princess Stardust. To Chevalia!

Your friend,
Pippa MacDonald

Don't miss Pippa's journey to find the golden horseshoes and save Chevalia!

Unicorn Princesses BY EMILY BLISS

Welcome to an
enchanted land ruled by
unicorn princesses!

Unicorn Princesses
SUNBEAM'S SHINE

Emily Bliss

Unicorn Princesses
FLASH'S DASH

Emily Bliss

Unicorn Princesses
BLOOM'S BALL

Emily Bliss

Unicorn Princesses
PRISM'S PAINT

Emily Bliss

Unicorn Princesses
BREEZE'S BLAST

Emily Bliss

Unicorn Princesses
MOON'S DANCE

Emily Bliss

COMING SOON!

www.bloomsbury.com
Facebook: KidsBloomsbury
Twitter: BloomsburyKids

Magic
Animal Rescue
BY E. D. BAKER

When magical creatures need help,
it's Maggie to the rescue!

www.bloomsbury.com
Facebook: KidsBloomsbury
Twitter: BloomsburyKids